Moonlight ◖ Editions

Grimm
How Six Men got on in the World

translated by Brian Alderson

Schocken Books · New York

Once upon a time there was a man who was skilled in many devices. He served in the wars and showed much daring and courage, but when the wars were over they gave him a fond farewell and three penn'orth of wages to see him on his way.

"Wait a minute," says he, "that's not good enough for me; once I get hold of the right people I shall see to it that the king hands over the treasures of his whole country." And full of anger he went off into the forest, where he saw a fellow standing who'd just pulled up six trees as if they were blades of corn.

"How would you like to serve me," he
says to him, "and travel along with me?"
"Fine," says the other, "but first of all I
must take home this little faggot of wood
for my mother," and he took one of the
trees, wound it round the five others, put
the faggot on his shoulder and carried it off.
Then he came back again and went off along

with his master who said, "The two of us should go far in the wide world."

After they'd gone along for a while they came to a huntsman kneeling down with his rifle levelled to take aim. The master says to him, "Huntsman what are you shooting at?" and the huntsman says:

"Two miles away there's a fly sitting on the branch of an oak-tree, I'm going to shoot him in the left eye."

"Oho! you must come with me!" says the man. "We three should go far together in the wide world." The huntsman was ready enough and went along with them till they

came to seven windmills whose sails were hurtling round even though there was no wind from east or west and not a leaf stirring on the trees.

Then the man says, "What on earth's driving these windmills, there's no sign of a breeze," and he went on a bit with his servants and after they'd walked a couple of miles they saw a fellow sitting in a tree

holding one nostril and blowing through the other.

"Lordy me! what are you doing up there?" says the man, and the other fellow answers:

"Do you see – two miles over there, there are seven windmills, I'm blowing to make them go round."

"Oho! you must come with me," says the man. "We four should go far together in the wide world."

So the blower got down and went along

with them, and after a time they saw a chap
standing there on one leg with the other
unclipped and lying on the ground beside
him. So the master says, "You look to have
made yourself very comfortable."

"Ah, I'm the runner," says the other,
"and I've unclipped that leg so that I shan't
leap off too quickly. When I run with two
legs it's faster than a bird flying."

"Oho! you must come with me. We five
should go far together in the wide world."

So he went along with them and it wasn't long before they met a fellow wearing a hat, but tilted right over one ear. So the master says to him, "Manners! manners! don't hang your hat on one ear like that, you look a right tomfool."

"Ooh I daren't do that," says the other,

"for if I put my hat straight there'll be a great frost and the birds'll freeze in the sky and fall down dead to the ground."

"Oho! you must come with me," says the master. "We six should go far together in the wide world."

So the six of them went to a city where the king had made it known that whoever raced with his daughter and beat her should marry her; but if he lost then he'd lose his head. So the man presented himself and said, "But I want one of my servants to do the running for me", to which the king answered, "Then you've pledged his life too. Your head and his head against victory."

Well, when it was all fixed and settled, the man clipped on the runner's other leg and said to him, "Now get a move on and see that we win."

It had to be agreed that whoever was the first to bring some water from a distant well should be the winner. So the runner got a pitcher and the king's daughter got another and they both set off running at the same time. But within a moment, with the princess only a few steps on her way, there wasn't an onlooker who could see anything of the runner – it was like nothing so much as the wind tearing by. In no time at all he'd got to the well, filled up the pitcher with water and turned back home. But half way back he was overcome with weariness, so he set down the pitcher, lay down on the ground and went to sleep. But he'd been careful to use a horse's skull that was lying there for a pillow so that he'd have a hard head-rest and would wake up pretty soon.

Meanwhile the princess, who was a good runner (good that is, for an ordinary mortal), had reached the well and was hurrying back with her pitcher full of water. But when she saw the runner lying there, she was overjoyed and said, "The enemy is delivered into my hands," and she tipped up his pitcher and ran on.

Well all would have been lost there and then had not the huntsman with the sharp eyes fortunately been standing up atop the castle, watching all that had been going on.

"That princess shan't get us that way," he said, loaded his rifle and fired with such skill that he shot the horse's skull from under the runner's head without doing him the least harm. The runner woke up at once, jumped in the air and saw that his pitcher was empty and the princess already far ahead. But he didn't despair. He ran back to the well with his pitcher, filled up with a fresh lot of water and was back home a good ten minutes before the princess. "See here," said he, "that made me lift my legs; it wasn't worth calling a race to start with."

Naturally it upset the king (and it upset his daughter a good deal more) that she should be carried off by a common soldier, and a discharged one at that; so they put their heads together to decide how they could be rid of him and all his companions.

"Don't worry," said the king. "I've found the means. They won't be coming back home again." And to them he said, "Well, gentlemen, you must all get together for a celebration. Eat! Drink!" and he led them to a room with a floor made of iron, and with iron doors and iron bars fixed over the windows.

A table had been put in this room, laid with rich foods, and the king said to them, "Go on in; enjoy yourselves." But once they were inside he had the doors locked and bolted. Then he sent for the cook and ordered him to get a furnace going under the room till the iron grew red-hot.

Well the cook did all that so that the six fellows in the room, sitting round the table, began to feel pretty warm and they thought it must be from eating. But as the heat got worse and worse and they tried to get out and found the doors and windows bolted they realised that the king's intentions had

not been of the best and that he was out to suffocate them.

"He won't get away with that," said the chap with the hat, "I'll raise such a frost that the fire'll feel ashamed of itself and creep away."

And he put his hat straight on his head and straight away there fell a frost that drove off all the heat and made the plates and the food begin to freeze.

So now – after a few hours had passed and the king thought them all shrivelled up – he had the door opened and went to look at them himself. But when the door swung wide there stood all six, sound in wind and limb, saying how glad they were to be able to get out and warm themselves because the

food was all frozen to the plates on account of the fearful cold.

Full of rage, the king went down to the cook and grabbed him by the shirt and demanded to know why he hadn't carried out his orders. The cook, though, answered, "It's hot enough there, see for yourself." And the king saw a huge, great fire was roaring beneath the iron room and he realised that he couldn't come at the six in that way.

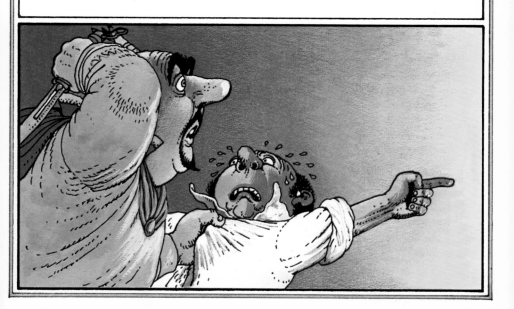

Now the king began to think of new ways to be rid of his hated guests. He summoned their master and said, "If you'll take gold instead of my daughter you shall have as much as you want."

"Indeed yes, Lord King," he answered, "if you'll give me as much as my servants can carry I'll not be after your daughter any more." The king was satisfied with that, and the man went on, "So I'll come back in a fortnight and fetch the gold." Then he called up all the tailors throughout the kingdom and had them sitting down for fourteen days sewing a sack. And when it was done the strong man who could tear up trees had to take the sack over his shoulder and go to the king.

Then the king said, "Who's that hefty fellow with a bale of canvas on his shoulder as big as a house?" He was properly

shocked and said to himself, "How much gold is he going to drag away?" Then he called for a ton of gold, which was brought in by sixteen of his strongest men, but the strong man grasped it with one hand, poked it in the sack and said, "Why don't you bring as much again? That lot hardly covers the bottom."

And so gradually the king had all his treasure brought out, and the strong man stowed it all in the sack and the sack still wasn't half full. "More!" he cried. "More! these few bits won't fill anything." So seven thousand wagons full of gold had to be driven in from all parts of the kingdom, and the strong man stowed these into his sack with the oxen and their harnesses and all.

"I won't keep much of an eye on it," he said. "I'll take what comes, just to get the sack full." And when everything was packed in, there was still room for more, but he said, "Enough's enough; people tie sacks up when they're not properly full,"

and he humped it on his back and set off
with his comrades.

Now when the king saw how this one
single man was carting off the whole
kingdom's wealth he was furious and
ordered out his cavalry. They had orders to
hunt down the six and seize the sack from
the strong man. So it was that two

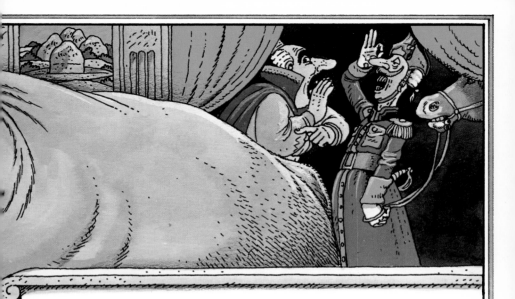

regiments soon overtook them and called
out to them, "You are prisoners! Lay down
the sack of gold or you'll all be hacked to
pieces!"

"What's that you say?" said the
nose-blower. "We're prisoners? Better to
say you're all going dancing on air!" And he
closed one nostril and blew at the two
regiments through the other, and they all
fluttered away into the blue sky, some that
way, some this.

    One sergeant-major cried
for mercy – he'd had nine wounds and was a
brave fellow who didn't deserve such
disgrace. So the nose-blower eased off a bit
so that he came down to earth again without
harm, and he said to him, "Very well, go
home to your king and tell him that if he'd
like to send some more cavalry I'd like to
blow them all up into the air."

When the king heard this news he said, "Let the fellows go, there's something about that lot." So the six companions brought home their riches, divided them up and lived contentedly to the end of their days.